The Three Billy Goats Gruff

Pictures by Stephen Carpenter

HarperFestival®
A Division of HarperCollinsPublishers

Once upon a time, there were three billy goats, and the name of all three billy goats was "Gruff."

The billy goats lived in a valley where there was very little grass, and they were very hungry. They wanted to go up the hillside to a meadow of green grass and daisies, where they could eat and eat and eat, and get fat.

But on the way up, there was a bridge over a river. And under the bridge lived a mean and ugly troll.

First, the youngest Billy Goat Gruff decided to cross the bridge.

"TRIP, TRAP! TRIP, TRAP!" went the bridge.

"Who's that tripping over my bridge?" roared the troll.

"Oh, it's only the tiniest little billy goat," said the first Billy Goat Gruff in his very small voice. "I'm on my way up the hillside, to make myself big and fat."

"No, you're not," said the troll, "for now I'm going to gobble you up!"

"Oh, please, don't eat me! I'm too little. Wait for the second billy goat. He's much bigger."

"Well, then, go ahead," said the troll.

After a while, the second Billy Goat Gruff came to cross the bridge.

"TRIP, TRAP, TRIP, TRAP, TRIP, TRAP!" went the bridge.

"Who's that tripping over my bridge?" roared the troll.

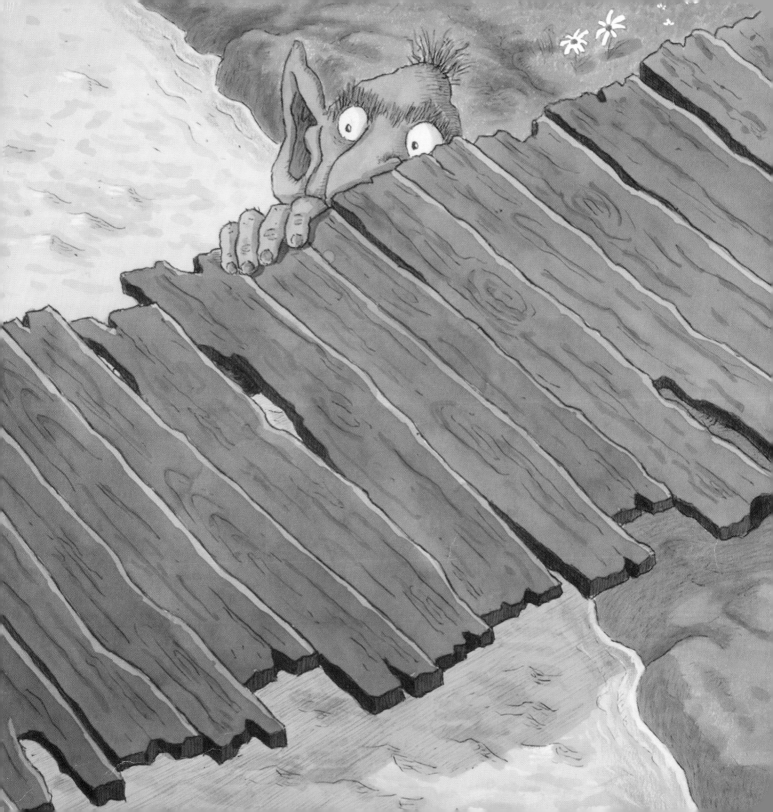

"It's the second Billy Goat Gruff, and I'm on my way up the hillside, to make myself big and fat," said the billy goat.

And his voice was not so small.

"No, you're not," said the troll, "for now I'm going to gobble you up!"

"Oh, please don't eat me! Wait for the third billy goat. He's much, much bigger."

"Well, then, go ahead," said the troll. And by now he was very hungry.

Just then, up came the third Billy Goat Gruff.
"TRIP, TRAP, TRIP, TRAP, TRIP, TRAP!"
went the bridge. The third billy goat was so heavy, the bridge
groaned and creaked under him.

"WHO'S THAT TRAMPING OVER MY BRIDGE?"
roared the troll.

"It is I, the third Billy Goat Gruff," cried the billy goat. And his voice was as big and loud as the troll's.

"At last!" said the troll. "Now I am coming to gobble you up!"

"Well, come along," cried the third Billy Goat Gruff. "I've got two big horns and four hard hooves, and I'm not afraid of you!"

So up climbed that mean, ugly troll, and the big billy goat butted him with his horns and stomped on him with his hooves, and tossed him off the bridge and into the river below.

Then he went up the hillside to join his brothers. In the meadow, the billy goats got so fat they were hardly able to walk home again. In fact, they are probably still there.

So snip, snap, snout,
This tale's told out!